ERRAND LASS

THERESA TOMLINSON
illustrations by
ANTHONY LEWIS

WALKER BOOKS
AND SUBSIDIARIES
LONDON · BOSTON · SYDNEY · AUCKLAND

This is a work of fiction. Names, characters, places and incidents
are either the product of the author's imagination or, if real,
are used fictitiously.

First published 2003 by Walker Books Ltd
87 Vauxhall Walk, London SE11 5HJ

2 4 6 8 10 9 7 5 3

Text © 2003 Theresa Tomlinson
Illustrations © 2003 Anthony Lewis

The right of Theresa Tomlinson to be identified as author
of this work has been asserted by her in accordance with the
Copyright, Designs and Patents Act 1988

This book has been typeset in Plantin

Printed in Great Britain by Cox & Wyman Ltd, Reading, Berkshire

British Library Cataloguing in Publication Data:
a catalogue record for this book
is available from the British Library

ISBN 0-7445-8321-7

www.walkerbooks.co.uk

Contents

Chapter 1

Mad Elaine

....

"Nice writing! I don't think!" The girl called
Samantha giggled and nudged her friend.

Maddy stared down at her page and
watched the line of scrawled letters she'd
written blur into nonsense. It was happening
again, all the b's had somehow turned
themselves the wrong way round so that they
looked like d's. Warmth crept into her cheeks
and she knew she was blushing.

The feeling was familiar; it had happened
before, just like this, in her old school. It had
got so bad there that she'd refused to go, and
it was only after four weeks of pretend
headaches and arguments and staying at
home bored that she'd allowed her mother to
persuade her that Upper Forge School might
be different.

She knew she couldn't change her horrible

spider-like writing without a fairy waving a magic wand, but she'd hoped the kids might not notice it straight away. She'd hoped they'd be kinder at Upper Forge, but those two who sat on the other side of her table kept giving each other swift meaningful looks and clapping their hands over their mouths to hide giggles. Maddy's heart sank.

"Hey!" Samantha tapped her pen onto Maddy's side of the table. "What did you say your name was?"

"Madeleine," Maddy said quietly. "Or Maddy for short."

There was silence again for a moment, then suddenly Amy, who had a pretty face and fair curly hair, snorted with laughter.

"What? What is it?" Samantha asked her.

But Amy collapsed onto her folder in giggles and couldn't get any words out.

Miss Taylor came over to them, frowning a little at the noise. "Can we all share the joke, Amy?" she asked.

"Nothing, Miss, nothing." Both Samantha

and Amy quickly dipped their heads over their work and started to write again, producing line after line of neat words.

Miss Taylor glanced down at Maddy's messy page, but smiled and touched her shoulder gently. "Keep going, Madeleine. First day in a new school is always a bit of a struggle, especially when you start in the middle of the term."

Maddy nodded and watched as Miss Taylor went on to the next table. She was OK; she was quite young and fashionable and so far she hadn't told her to "hurry up and make her work neater", or asked anyone to read aloud.

"Tell me!" Samantha whispered, nudging Amy's elbow. "Go on, tell me. What was the joke?"

Amy glanced across at Maddy, then quickly away again. "Can't," she smirked. "She'll hear."

"Whisper it – go on!"

Amy put her lips to Samantha's ear, though

her eyes flicked defiantly across to Maddy again. Samantha frowned at first, but then suddenly covered her mouth in silent mirth. Then at last she looked up, tapping the side of her head, a crazy expression on her face.

"Don't say it!" Amy begged, exploding with giggles again.

But Samantha wouldn't be stopped. "Mad Elaine!" she sniggered. "Get it? Good name for you. Mad Elaine! Because you're mad."

Maddy's pen stopped. It refused to budge. Her forehead prickled with sweat and her eyes blurred with hot tears. She blinked hard, determined that the girls weren't going to make her cry.

The buzzer went for morning break, bringing sudden relief.

Samantha and Amy flipped their books shut and jumped up from the table. "You ought to sit with the Muppet," Samantha told Maddy, then turned and walked away.

Miss Taylor came over to her as the classroom emptied. "Are you getting on all right?" she asked.

Maddy got up slowly from her place, shrugging her shoulders. She couldn't explain; there was no point in even trying, however nice Miss Taylor might be. It was bound to happen again and again, just the way it had at Grinders Hill School.

"Let's try sitting you somewhere else," Miss Taylor said brightly. "Let's move your things over here so that you can work with Michael. You'll be OK with Michael."

Maddy moved her things obediently and then went out into the yard. She kept well away from Samantha and Amy and it wasn't long before the buzzer was ordering them back to the classroom.

After break they did maths, which Maddy usually found slightly easier, but she had trouble getting the lines straight and hadn't brought a ruler with her.

Michael turned out to be a skinny little boy with glasses and ears that stuck out, who smiled shyly at her, but didn't even try to talk. He was left-handed and Maddy could see that he was constantly struggling not to smudge his numbers. When she glanced over at Samantha and Amy they waved at her from the other side of the room and then giggled again. It was quite clear that their smiling faces were not friendly at all.

She sighed and turned back to her work. Michael pushed his ruler into the middle of the table. "You can borrow it," he whispered.

"Thanks," said Maddy.

As she struggled with the next sum, he silently pushed a paper-wrapped toffee towards her.

"Thanks," she said again as she took the sweet.

Michael's round face suddenly lit up with a wide smile. Miss Taylor had been right; Maddy would be OK with Michael.

Then one of the boys walked past their table. "Muppet," he hissed and, with a hand movement that was so fast Maddy hardly saw it happen, he flicked one of Michael's ears.

Michael's face twisted with the sharpness of the pain. He rubbed his ear fiercely and his eyes watered, but he quickly recovered and smiled across at Maddy again. "They call me Muppet," he whispered.

"Are you all right?" she asked.

He nodded and carried on with his work.

Chapter 2

The Millennium Galleries

The afternoon was better, and for the last half hour the children were allowed to choose what they did. Maddy drew clothes designs with some new felt-tip pens Miss Taylor had offered her, and Michael helped himself to a box of technical Lego. Maddy drew a row of girls dressed in fashionable gear, while on the other side of the table Michael's fingers flew back and forth until a crane appeared, with astonishing detail.

"That's good," she told him.

"Mmm. Just can't make it work," he said. "Need a strong elastic band to use as a belt to link the drive shafts."

Maddy whipped off the silver elastic band that held her ponytail in place. "Here, try this."

"Ye-ah!" Michael cheered. Within moments

he had the crane working smoothly, a small handle winding the grabber up and down.

"Hey – look what the Muppet's done!"

Approval came from all around.

"That's good, Muppet."

"Hey, Muppet, that's cool."

Michael smiled again.

Just before they went home Miss Taylor gave out all sorts of information about a school trip that had been planned for Friday. "The coach is coming at nine to pick us up, so everyone must be here early. We hope to be at the Millennium Galleries by ten. You must all bring packed lunches."

Maddy felt confused. She'd never remember all those instructions, and the thought of a day out with Samantha and Amy seemed pretty scary; just being at school was bad enough.

Miss Taylor caught her arm gently as the children were leaving. "How's it been?" she asked.

"Um… The afternoon was better."
Maddy tried hard to be polite, but she was
already thinking that a headache might have
to be invented for the outing on Friday
morning.

"Please give us a chance?" Miss Taylor
said. "I know that you weren't happy at your
last school, Maddy. And I know that you have
a bit of a problem with some things, but I
really want to help. Just give us a chance, will
you?"

Maddy nodded. How could she say no?

"I think you'll enjoy Friday. Have you been
to the new galleries yet?"

"No."

"They're full of wonderful silverware and
cutlery – things that made Sheffield famous."

Maddy couldn't think what to say. A
gallery full of cutlery didn't sound very
exciting.

"Why don't you take a sketch pad with
you?" Miss Taylor insisted. "You might find
something you'd like to draw."

"Mmm," Maddy murmured, faintly interested now.

"One thing I did notice about you..."

Maddy held her breath. What was coming now? she wondered.

"You're a fine artist, Madeleine, there's no doubt about that."

Maddy let out her breath and smiled. She went home feeling a little better. An outing with Samantha and Amy might be bad, but Miss Taylor calling her a fine artist was a different matter. She could certainly do with a bit more of that.

Maddy managed somehow to struggle through the week by keeping well away from Samantha and Amy and keeping her head down in Michael's company.

On Friday morning, the coach arrived on time and they all scrambled aboard. The nightmare of who to sit with was solved by Michael, who shyly patted the seat beside him as she came past. But Samantha and

Amy made the journey horrible by falling into the seat behind them and giggling all the way, murmuring stupid remarks like, "Mad Elaine's going to marry the Muppet!"

At last the coach pulled up outside the big modern gallery. Though she'd lived in Sheffield all her life, Maddy had never been in there before. Delicious smells came from the café, but Miss Taylor steered them straight up the huge escalator that loomed in front of the entrance. "Plenty of time to eat later," she said. "We're going to picnic in Orchard Square."

One of the galleries was showing a special exhibition about films. As they walked past they got glimpses of Star Wars stormtrooper suits, Dr Who's little metal dog K-9, and a uniform from Hogwarts School.

"Metalwork gallery first," Miss Taylor insisted. "I'll never get you out if we go into the film exhibition first."

The metalwork displays were more interesting than Maddy had expected.

She kept well away from Samantha and Amy, and sadly Michael too; she could do without giving anyone a reason to start teasing her.

Elaborately patterned silver teapots, cups and baskets were displayed in gleaming glass cases. One side of the room was lined with all sorts of strange-looking implements, with flaps that you could lift in front of them. The top of the flap gave a clue, like NO WET WHISKERS WITH ME, and then when you lifted the flap it told you what the object was – a special moustache-protecting spoon. CUT AND DUNK was a boiled egg topper and EAT YOUR GREENS was a special pea-eating knife, with a groove to line up all the peas so that you could shovel them into your mouth.

Miss Taylor started reading them herself and then asked her pupils to read them out loud. Maddy backed away from the group, her stomach suddenly churning; she mustn't be the next to be asked. Everyone else gathered round, lifting the flaps up and down, trying to guess what the objects were and laughing as the suggestions got crazier and crazier.

Chapter 3

Chapter 3

Butter Girls, Nutter Girls

....

As Maddy wandered away from the jostling
and laughter, a lifelike oil painting high on
the side wall caught her eye. She looked more
closely to see the bold brush strokes. The
picture showed two young women wearing
greyish overalls, red headscarves tied round
their heads and necks. One of the women
stared boldly out of the picture, straight at
Maddy it seemed, while the other looked
away, her hand on her hip and a very
determined expression on her face.

"Ooh, you wouldn't mess with them!" an
old man chuckled as he walked past.

Maddy looked after him, puzzled.

The man smiled at her surprise and came
back. "We used to keep out of their way when
I was young. If we saw them coming,
marching through town arm in arm, all

shouting and laughing together, we'd scarper, we would, I can tell you!"

"Who are they?" Maddy asked.

The man didn't explain, but pointed to a label beneath the picture. "Oh, tough lot, they were," he said as he walked away. "You met them round every street corner in Sheffield when I were a lad – bold as brass, they were!"

Maddy looked at the label; she thought it said BUTTER GIRLS.

"Butter Girls?" she murmured, still puzzled. "Were they girls who made butter?"

"Butter Girls! Did you hear that? Butter Girls!" Samantha was standing behind her. She and Amy burst out giggling. "Butter Girls! What a nutter girl!"

Then as Maddy looked hard again at the label, she saw that she'd misread it. BUFFER GIRLS was what it really said.

Maddy turned away from the picture at once, feeling stupid, her cheeks flaring hot and crimson. She could have kicked herself for making such a silly mistake, but the really dreadful thing was letting Samantha and Amy know about it.

The terrible embarrassment of it all made her feel faint and a bit dizzy; she put out a hand to steady herself against the glass case in front of her. The glass was cool and solid and made her feel a little better. As she lifted her head she saw the reflection of the picture in the glass. She could see Samantha and Amy still standing in front of it. Seeing the picture like that was strange because she couldn't make out the frame very clearly, and it almost looked as though her two tormentors were standing there beneath two real buffer girls.

And then it happened. Maddy rubbed her eyes, because they seemed to be playing bad tricks on her again. She could have sworn that the two buffer girls had turned their heads to look at each other, then turned again to stare sternly down at Samantha and Amy.

"Well, Iris!" Maddy froze at the sound of a rough voice. "I'm damn sure I wouldn't put up wi' that, would you?"

Where had that voice come from? Maddy wondered. There was nobody else near them now.

Then another girl's voice replied. "I would not, Hilda! Right cheeky little madams! I wouldn't put up wi' none o' that nonsense!"

Maddy spun round, her eyes wide and her heart beating. But the picture was exactly as it had been. The two buffer girls stood there, frozen in time, in their wooden frame.

A shiver ran down her back and her hot cheeks turned suddenly cold and clammy. Had that really happened?

"What's up with you?" Samantha demanded. "Come on, Aym! I told you she was mad! Miss Taylor says we can go on to the film bit now."

"Nutter girl!" Amy whispered, moving quickly away like she was Samantha's shadow.

Maddy just stood there for a few minutes after they'd gone, staring up at the picture, trying to get over the shock, and glad that her classmates had all gone off to see the other exhibition. What was going on? She wasn't just seeing things; she was hearing things too.

With shaking hands she pulled her sketch pad out of her bag and set about furiously drawing the buffer girls. She had to get them down on paper – the bold stare of one and the determined chin of the other. When at last she stopped and held her sketch up in front of her, she felt much better. Her drawing wasn't perfect, but she had managed to produce something that was quite recognizable.

She was the only school-kid left in the room and realized that she really ought to catch the others up. But then she noticed that on a little stand underneath the picture was something that looked oddly like a metal phone. It was a speaker that you could hold to your ear, and there was a choice of three buttons to press, to hear recordings giving information about the picture.

She smiled. That was it! She wasn't going mad after all. That must have been what she'd heard – a bit of one of the recordings. She picked up the speaker and pressed the top button, but that message was nothing like the voices she'd heard before. It was a man's voice talking about the hard and dirty work that Sheffield buffer girls used to do. He described how they stood at buffing wheels, polishing forks and spoons, constantly throwing handfuls of oily sand onto their work.

The second message seemed to be much more likely. It was definitely a woman's voice speaking, but as Maddy tried to listen a little boy came up behind her and started banging the information flaps up and down. She couldn't hear what was being said at all.

She looked around at him impatiently. Where was his mother? Couldn't one of the gallery staff come and tell him to be quiet?

"There you are, Madeleine!" It was Miss Taylor looking in at her from the doorway. "It's almost twelve o'clock; time for our picnic," she said, glancing worriedly at her watch. "You have seen the film display, haven't you?"

Maddy felt too foolish to explain what she'd really been doing, but Miss Taylor came towards her and her eyes settled on Maddy's drawing. "Ooh, now then, just look at that – it's wonderful! That's going on the classroom wall first thing on Monday morning. Could I take it? I'll put it in my folder to make sure it doesn't get creased."

"Yes, of course." Maddy was pleased to be praised again.

"Now, we must hurry and catch up with the others," Miss Taylor insisted. "So glad it's such a fine day and everyone's behaving so well."

"Hmm," Maddy murmured. With a worried backward glance towards the painting, she followed her teacher out of the gallery.

Chapter 4

Orchard Square

··

When Maddy and Miss Taylor arrived in the square, most of the class had found themselves a space on a bench and were already rifling in their bags for sandwiches and packets of crisps.

"I'm starving!"

"Hey, that's my drink you've got!"

"Ooh – I bit my tongue!"

"You don't have your chocolate mousse first!"

"I do!"

Orchard Square was a good place for a picnic: a pedestrian area with seats, surrounded by lively shops, but well away from supertrams and traffic. Maddy could see that there was space to sit next to Michael, but she ignored him and sat down next to her teacher.

She'd no sooner pulled out her own bag of crisps when she jumped at the sudden *ding-dong, ding-dong* from the clock tower that announced it was quarter to twelve.

"Here they come! Here they come!"

Whispers of anticipation rose from all around. Everyone knew what was going to happen and it wasn't really much of a surprise; it was something that all Sheffield children had seen time and time again, but somehow it still made people jump and smile.

As soon as the clock had finished ringing its set of bells, two triangular wooden cupboards, high up in the wall of the clock tower, opened with a creak and a great chugging sound. Then out of the cupboards swung two painted wooden figures: a buffer girl and a grinder.

The grinder man tilted forwards holding his work out to his wheel, and every time he did it a great whining metallic sound arose. Little children shrieked and pointed. Older children who'd seen it many times before just watched, grinning. Grown-ups sitting out in the sun at the café tables ignored it and carried on with their conversations.

The buffer girl bent to her work twice, but then with a slightly jerky movement she pulled back and turned her head as though she was looking down at the crowd of milling shoppers below her. Then suddenly it was over; the figures swung back inside their cupboards and the doors closed firmly behind them.

"Buffer girls everywhere today," Miss Taylor commented in a chatty way.

Maddy nodded. "Yes, there are," she agreed politely. She felt safe sitting beside this teacher; maybe she should try harder to make herself settle down and feel OK at Upper Forge School.

It was pleasant sitting in Orchard Square in the warm sun, watching people go by. A thin young man with long hair drawn back in a ponytail was singing and dancing and trying to sell the *Big Issue*. Everyone was laughing as they went by and some stopped to buy a copy. Two young women with toddlers and babies in pushchairs flopped down to rest on the nearby seats, quickly giving in to their children's pleas for ice creams. Men in suits strode past, briefcases in their hands, speaking to invisible people, mobile phones clutched to their ears. A clown with a red nose and bright stripy clothes came out of a sweet shop giving out balloons and tiny packets of jelly babies.

"Over here! Over here!" Samantha was on her feet in a moment, waving like mad at the clown.

Miss Taylor shook her head. "Samantha, you're too old for that!"

But the clown pranced over to where they sat and started giving them balloons and sweets. Maddy smiled and watched. It almost felt like being at the seaside, which was a strange thought when really she was in the middle of a big industrial city. Then she saw that the hands on the clock at the top of the tower were nearly together. For once she was determined that she wouldn't be surprised when the bells rang out. There were steps leading to a higher gallery of shops, and Maddy realized that if you went up those steps you could lean out over the rail and find yourself just beneath the grinder and the buffer girl.

She turned to Miss Taylor. "Is it OK if I go up the steps?" she asked.

Miss Taylor looked puzzled for a moment, but then she seemed to understand. "Sure!" she nodded. "Just don't go where I can't see you. I don't want any lost children today!"

Maddy got up and raced up the steps. Something made her feel that she had to get there before the clock struck twelve. She managed it and stood there staring up at the two triangular cupboards, lovely smells rising up to her from the herb shop directly below.

Then it all started: *ding-dong, ding-dong, ding-dong, ding-dong*. After that came the *dong, dong, dong* of the deepest bell announcing the hour. As it was twelve o'clock the chimes went on for a long time. Then as soon as the twelfth *dong* sounded, and with a loud creak above her head, the doors began to open. The chugging sounds were heard and the buffer girl seemed to swing and judder as she appeared.

Standing there just below felt very different; the figures were more lifelike, the expressions clear on their faces. Maddy saw what she'd never noticed before: that a small black cat sat in a basket at the buffer girl's feet. The grinder worked at his wheel and the buffer girl turned her head to look down at the shoppers. The cat turned its head too and Maddy thought that in among the metallic sounds of the grinding she could hear the cat miaow. Then as the buffer girl's head swung round, Maddy had the strangest feeling that the painted wooden face looked straight at her and seemed amused and surprised to see her there.

"She really did see me!" Maddy muttered.

The shock of it made her stomach lurch, but then the two figures vanished from sight and both the doors closed behind them.

Chapter 5

Worse Than Ever

....

Maddy stared up at the closed doors.

"Don't be so daft," she told herself.

Then she heard a shrieking laugh from just below and knew that things were about to get worse. She looked down from the gallery to see that Samantha and Amy were standing beneath her and watching her from outside the herbal store.

"Did you hear that?" Samantha yelled pointing up at her. "She's talking to the wooden figures!"

"Nutter girl! Nutter girl! Mad Elaine!" Amy chanted.

Once again Maddy felt beads of sweat prickling her forehead as she turned hot with embarrassment. She looked down over the railings and saw that all her new classmates were now staring up at her and Miss Taylor, too, was looking a little anxious. Maddy had an almost uncontrollable urge to turn around and run and hide in the bookshop that had an open door onto the gallery just behind her. But there was nothing else to do except swallow her pride and go back down to join them. She walked slowly down the steps, trying to breathe calmly while Samantha giggled wildly. As she reached the bottom Miss Taylor glanced at her watch and said that it was time for them all to get back on the bus. Maddy sighed with relief.

As they left Orchard Square, she looked back at the clock tower, but what she saw there made her feel worse than ever. This problem with seeing things the wrong way round was getting serious, for she thought she saw the hands on the clock steadily moving backwards. She was used to seeing things the wrong way round, but she'd never seen anything like this.

She trembled a little as she heaved her schoolbag onto her shoulder. That's not right, she thought. Those clock hands looked as though they were turning back time.

Maddy was relieved to get home that day. When her mother asked her how the trip had gone, she shook her head fiercely. "Horrible, horrible," she said.

Her mother sighed, knowing that this would mean another headache and a hard struggle to get her to go to school on Monday morning.

"Well – it wasn't all horrible," Maddy admitted, trying to be fair. "The teacher's OK and some of the kids are OK and … the Millennium Galleries are good."

Her mother came and sat down beside her. "Well, that doesn't sound too bad. I haven't seen those galleries properly myself yet."

Maddy looked across at her mother. "Can we go tomorrow? I can show you all the things that I saw. I didn't get to see the film exhibition properly."

Her mother looked surprised.

"Tomorrow?" Then she smiled. "OK, why not? I've a bit of shopping to do and I can do it in town while we're there."

When they arrived at the gallery on Saturday morning, Maddy stopped herself from racing straight to the buffer girls picture and went into the film exhibition first. It was interesting, with all sorts of buttons to press and things to do. Her mother got all dreamy-eyed as she watched clips from films that had been popular when she was young. Maddy enjoyed it, but she got impatient in the end and left her mother staring up at David Essex, who was singing and dancing in a clownlike costume that didn't appeal to her at all.

"I'll be in the metalwork gallery," she whispered in her mother's ear.

Maddy found herself looking up at the painting of the two buffer girls again. She lifted the speaker to her ear and carefully pressed the button for the recording, which she hadn't yet heard properly. A woman's voice started speaking but, though she listened all the way through, Maddy couldn't find those rough voices that had seemed to be giving her advice the day before.

"They've got to be here somewhere," she muttered, pressing the button again. She listened once more and thought she did hear the voices this time, but they were saying something quite different.

"Half past eight and there's not sight nor sound o' her!"

"Eeh dear – the Missus will have summat to say about it. Daft lass – this is no way to start a job o' work!"

These voices were loud, almost as if they were right inside her head. Maddy took the speaker away from her ear and put it back on the stand, though she kept a tight hold on it. What happened next filled her with panic – the voices continued, even though the speaker was nowhere near her ear. They really were inside her head!

"Hark at that, is that her now? I thought I heard someone out there in the yard."

"Is that the new lass? If it is, tha'd best get theesen here quick as a flash before the Missus comes."

Maddy shivered; she must be going mad like Samantha said. She closed her eyes for a moment, feeling dizzy, just as she had the day before, but she still gripped the phone-like speaker tight. Then something even more frightening happened: the smooth metal seemed to move in her hand, heating up just a little and turning rough and gritty. She opened her eyes in alarm and saw that it was no longer a modern speaker she was holding onto, but a handle, with a heavy black latch beneath it. The handle was set into double doors, very worn and painted green. Maddy's heart began beating fast as she looked frantically about her; the huge modern gallery had vanished from sight and instead she was standing in a cobbled yard.

Chapter 6

Missus Lily

"I shouldn't stand faffing about out there, lass!"

Maddy was frozen stiff with terror. What on earth had happened to her?

"Come on in!" the familiar rough voice shouted. "Come on in, lass. We'll not bite thee, will we, Iris? Not very hard, anyway!"

Maddy couldn't do anything else but lift the heavy latch and walk in. The place stank of oil and metal, rather like a garage, and as the doors swung open she saw a workshop, with wheels set into a heavy workbench. Each wheel was linked to belts that stretched up to a drive shaft near the ceiling. A gang of young women were pulling on grubby overalls and pinning aprons made of brown paper over the top. They covered their hair with familiar red scarves.

"Wey-hey! Here she is at last!"

"Get thissen in here, Mary! What time do tha call this? Missus Lily will be here any moment. Tha should've got the fire going by now!"

"But I'm not Mary, I'm Maddy!"

"Oh, well – we was told Mary. If this were one o' t'big places tha'd be locked out for being late and earn nowt!"

"O lor, Hilda! Look at the clothes they send 'em out in nowadays. Has tha got buff brats?"

Maddy stood there open-mouthed, quite unable to speak. She could only shake her head.

"Hilda, let her borrow one o' yours for today. She don't look old enough to be out working, she's nowt but a brat herssen. Missus Lily'll have her for breakfast!"

"Here, Mary, get this on!" A girl who was a bit older than Maddy, but quite small in stature, held out one of the overalls. "Quick as yer can, into these buff brats. I'm

-58-

supposed to be starting on t'spindle today, and I've just got a minute or two to tell yer what's what! Iris, will you help?"

Maddy was horrified, but the bossy way they talked made her do as she was told. How could she begin to explain to them? Something very scary had happened to her and she wasn't sure what.

She found herself bundled helplessly into the large overall that they called a buff brat. They fastened her up at the back and whipped a red rag around her head, tying it with a knot. The big woman called Iris slapped a sheet of brown paper around one of Maddy's legs and started fastening it on with string.

"No!" she protested.

"Oh, yes," Iris insisted, quickly moving on to the other leg. "We all have the same. Your legs'll be black without brown paper leggings."

Maddy saw that their legs were covered with brown paper in just the same way.

"Now this, to keep the muck out," Hilda said, tying another rag around Maddy's neck.

"Right," said Iris. "Now tha looks the business, we must get to work. Tha'd best leave the fire for now and get the sand topped up."

Just then the door swung open again and a plump woman with a round face came in. She wore a long brown dress and a cream straw hat. She took a quick glance around the place. "Should be at work by now," she told them sharply.

"Just setting the new lass up, Missus Lily," Hilda explained.

All the women moved quickly towards the workbench and settled themselves at the buffing wheels. They picked up spoons in one hand and sand in the other, then set to work, polishing the spoons with the spindles that stuck out at the side of the wheels. As the spoons touched the leather buffs, which whizzed round on the end of the spindles, they made a high, grating whine.

"You two get going," Missus Lily told Iris and Hilda. "I'll see to the errand lass."

"But— I'm not—" Maddy tried.

"We don't have any buts in my buffing shop." Missus Lily rounded on her fiercely, setting her hat aside and tying an apron around herself. "You do exactly as I say. I'll tell you once, but I won't tell you twice, so listen well! First, top up the sand!"

She pointed to a metal bucket that was filled with oily sand and had a small shovel stuck in it. "That's right, pick it up. Now go round to each lass and add a shovelful to their pile. Quick – this should have been done before they started!"

There was nothing for it but to set to work. The bucket of sand was heavy, but as Maddy did the rounds the lasses grinned at her, and some of them winked.

"She's not as bad as she seems!" Hilda mouthed at her. Maddy couldn't hear much above the whine of the machinery.

As they worked, the gritty sand flew all

over the place and soon their hands and faces were filthy. Maddy quickly saw why they dressed as they did and, when a shower of oily sand flew over her shoulders, she was grateful that they'd made her do the same.

"Quickly, quickly!" Missus Lily called. "Get the fire going now!"

Hilda grinned at her and bent close to shout in her ear. "Don't let her get yer down, Mary. Stand yer ground! You'll be all right! I laid the fire last night!"

Maddy turned back to the Missus. Standing up to her was easier said than done.

"Come on, lass. Shift yerssen." Missus Lily was tapping her foot, hands on hips, her face unsmiling. "This should be done before they start. Tomorrow I'll expect to find it all ready, matches there!"

Tomorrow morning? She wouldn't be here tomorrow morning! Not if she could help it. Maddy saw with gratitude that the fire was neatly laid with rolled newspaper tucked in at the bottom and sticks and coals on top.

She struck a match and carefully lit the newspaper, standing back to watch as the flames licked about the sticks.

"No time for larking! Fetch more coals!" Missus Lily wasn't giving her a minute to rest. "Fill the kettle, set it to boil. Now then, take more work to the lasses! I don't want to see any of those piles o' spoons looking small."

Maddy heaved a big wooden box up off the floor and was soon going round the workbench again, dishing out roughly made spoons to the women, while the Missus inspected their work, pointing out flaws in the finished spoons that needed to be done again.

"Hurry up, Mary," the lasses mouthed at her as she went round. "Fetch us our tea."

"They're asking for tea," she nervously told the Missus.

"Aye, well, they will be. It's thy fault they're late in getting it. Best get teapot warmed and kettle poured."

"Where are the cups, please?" she asked.

"Cups?" Missus Lily raised her eyebrows. "They've all got their own mugs – take the teapot round to them. They drink it while they work."

Maddy had never worked like this before; her shoulders, back and legs ached. She longed for a rest – didn't these buffer lasses ever stop? They drank their tea standing at the wheels as they continued to work away.

When, at last, she put the empty teapot down on the table she saw something that confirmed all her worst fears. On the grubby whitewashed wall above the table were pinned photographs of the buffer lasses on a beach and on swingboats. They were pinned all round a calendar. She squinted at the page. The numbers at the top of it jumped about in front of her eyes – nothing but ones and nines. The year was nineteen hundred and nineteen!

Chapter 7

Off Round Town

....

"No time for gawping!" Missus Lily was after
her again. "Go round all t'lasses and ask if
they want their dinners heating up."

Maddy went straight to Hilda and bellowed
in her ear, "Where do I heat up food?"

Hilda laughed. "In t'side oven, o' course!
Eeh dear, we've got a right one here – she
knows nowt."

"Aye – but she's learning fast, I can see
that," Iris shouted with a wink across from
the next buffing wheel.

Maddy saw the small black door beside the
fire and felt foolish; of course she should have
known that. She went round the girls and
collected pies, pasties and little pots of stew;
the buffer lasses certainly weren't going to
starve. She was struggling to get the dishes
inside the oven when the Missus started

again. "Now then, Mary, after they've eaten their dinner, you wash up and then you set about cutting out the aprons. That's your job every afternoon – are you listening to me, lass?"

It was too much; Maddy's thoughts were in total confusion. Her chin trembled as though she was going to burst into tears, but then she remembered what Hilda had said: "Stand yer ground!" She wasn't even meant to be here working so hard for them! She wasn't just confused now; she was getting angry.

"I can't..." she said. Her face was red from the heat of the oven as she struggled to her feet. "I can't listen to what you're saying and get this food in the oven all at the same time! I can't do two things at once! I just can't!"

She slammed the oven door with a bang and turned round to face the Missus. What would happen now? she wondered.

But when Maddy dared to look up she was very surprised to see that Missus Lily's big mouth had curved into a wide smile.

"Fair enough, my darlin'!" she chuckled, leaning back and placing her huge hands on her hips. "Don't get yourself upset like that. Tha's doing fine and shaping up good and proper. Come and sit thissen down for a minute and have a cup o' tea."

Suddenly all the lasses were laughing at her and shaking their heads, while Maddy went to sit down as she was told. The Missus patted her shoulder, then let her borrow her own mug and poured tea for her.

Maddy's hands were shaking as she held the mug, but slowly she began to feel much better as she sat there sipping the warm drink. Gorgeous smells came from the oven, cutting through the oily stink of the workshop, making her realize that she was very hungry.

When the clock on the wall struck half past twelve, the buffing wheels were stopped, and a sudden silence fell on the place; although it didn't last for long.

The Missus brought a bucket of water and

the lasses chattered and laughed as they washed their hands. She gave Maddy a wink. "This is your job tomorrow, Errand Lass," she said.

Maddy could see what Hilda meant about Missus Lily; she wasn't as bad as she seemed. But still her head was full of worrying thoughts – would she be here tomorrow? Where would she go when they all went home at night? Could she ever get home again?

The buffer lasses pulled their hot food from the oven and settled themselves to eat, smacking their lips and blowing on their fingers. It wasn't long before they realized that their new errand lass had nothing, so they found a clean bowl and put contributions into it. Maddy felt like a beggar, but they laughed away her protests.

"No one works here and goes home with an empty belly," said Iris, patting her own large one.

As soon as they'd finished they were up on

their feet again. "Who's off round town?" asked Hilda.

With a sigh Maddy gathered together the dirty dishes, eyeing the bucket of water rather unhappily. She suspected that was her washing-up bowl.

"Hey," said Hilda, "this is yer dinner break, Mary – even errand lasses get half an hour off! Leave those till we start again, come on, we're off round town!"

Maddy looked for approval from the Missus, but she was sitting comfortably with the older women drinking tea. She found herself grabbed from either side by Hilda and Iris, and before she could say anything they were off walking arm in arm, out of the workshop, through the yard and up the street.

Going outside was a terrible shock, for Sheffield did not look like Sheffield at all. The place seemed to be crammed with little workshops. The clatter of clogs could be heard everywhere as people in grimy work clothes walked through the streets.

The buildings were unrecognizable at first, then suddenly Maddy caught her breath as she saw the familiar town hall.

"Down here." Hilda hauled her round the corner. "We go to Mary Langley's for our spice."

Maddy looked back for the huge Central Library building, but something called a music hall was there in its place. As they turned the corner into another street she saw the familiar Lyceum Theatre in all its glory, looking much the same as it had when she'd gone to see the pantomime last Christmas. There was no sign of the Crucible Theatre, but a huge fancy building called the Theatre Royal stood just across the road from the Lyceum.

The lasses went into a small sweet shop that said MARY LANGLEY CONFECTIONER over the doorway. The place was crammed with row upon row of jars filled with brightly coloured sweets, and it smelled like heaven. They bought a mixed bag of Pontefract cakes, humbugs, lemon and chocolate drops, and made Maddy try them all.

Then once they'd got their "spice" they were off again, marching through the centre of a bustling, smoky city that just now and then seemed a little bit familiar. They marched up Fargate, dodging funny bus-like trams that ran on metal rails, with overhead cables that sparked as the trams rattled past. Men high up on ladders, checking the cables, shouted cheekily down at the lasses, who made rude signs back at them.

Maddy was sure that they would soon be at Orchard Square, but however hard she looked she could see no sign of the entrance.

Other buffer gangs shouted greetings and insults and nobody looked surprised at the girls strolling past the shops in their dirty buff brats. There seemed to be a small cinema on every street corner and the lasses stopped at each one to stare at the film advertisements.

"Oh, look at Charlie! He does make me laugh!" Iris pointed at photographs of Charlie

Chaplin with his bowler hat and black moustache.

"Oh, no, Rudolph's my favourite!" Hilda smiled dreamily at the photograph of the handsome young Rudolph Valentino, who was wearing quite a lot of make-up.

All too soon the hands on the town hall clock were warning them to rush back to the workshop. As the clock struck one, the buffing wheels started turning again and each lass was back at work, oily sand flying everywhere, hands caked with dirt.

Maddy washed up in the bucket, just as she'd expected to. Then the Missus got her cutting out brown paper aprons for the next day. "I'll cut you one so you can use it as a pattern," she said.

Maddy watched carefully and decided that this job wasn't so bad; at least you could sit down to do it. As the afternoon wore on the lasses started singing all the latest songs from the films they'd seen. Maddy sat beside the fire listening to them and cutting out apron shapes while the Missus nodded approval. "Tha's a dab hand at that," she said.

Maddy made more tea, which the lasses drank as they worked; there were no tea breaks, it seemed. Then, just as Maddy was about to fall asleep by the fire, the wheels stopped and the lasses shouted at her for more water to wash in. They started to change their clothes and helped Maddy out of her buff brats. What am I going to do now? she wondered.

But just at that moment the workshop doors flew open and a young girl rushed in. "I'm terrible sorry," she announced, "but my mam was took ill and I had to fetch the doctor and look after the little uns! I would never have missed my first day for anything else."

They all looked at her puzzled. "Who are you?" Missus Lily asked the girl.

Now it was her turn to look surprised. "I'm Mary, your new errand lass – didn't my auntie fix it all up with you?"

Suddenly every pair of eyes in the buffing shop turned on Maddy. She'd had some terrible moments in her life, but nothing had ever been quite as dreadful as this.

Chapter 8

Chapter 8

A Special Prize

··

The buffer lasses stood with their hands on their hips, staring angrily at Maddy. "Who are *you*, then?" demanded Missus Lily.

"What's tha playing at?"

"Damned cheek, I say."

"I said she were far too young!"

"I said she knew nowt!"

Maddy had had enough. She threw her buff brats and head-rag on the floor and marched over to the door, her face red with anger. All shame and embarrassment had fled as she turned to face them.

"I tried to explain, but you wouldn't give me a chance. I told you I was Maddy, not Mary, but none of you would listen. You've got a cheek, you have – all of you. I've done a good day's work for you, without pay. You lot have got nothing to complain about!"

There was a moment of silence, but then suddenly they started laughing and nodding their heads in agreement. They slapped each other on the back, shaking with laughter, waving and blowing kisses to Maddy.

"Quite right, darlin'! You are quite right!" said Iris.

Maddy grabbed hold of the rough door handle. It was the handle she'd found herself holding when she'd first arrived in that harsh place. Was it the handle that had somehow brought her here? she thought suddenly. Could it take her back again? Surely that must be it?

The buffer lasses continued to laugh, but Maddy gripped the handle tightly, closing her eyes and taking a deep breath. She felt the palm of her hand grow warm and tingly, and when she opened her eyes again something strange was certainly happening. The lasses were still there and they were still laughing, but she could only see them as though through misted glass. She closed her eyes once more and this time she felt the rough handle turn smooth.

"Yes!" she murmured.

When she peeped again she saw that the shiny metal speaker gleamed in her palm, looking just like a modern phone. Missus Lily and her lasses had vanished; the familiar painting of the two buffer girls was hanging above her once again.

Maddy sighed with relief; she was back in the Millennium Galleries and not trapped for ever in that smelly, dirty, hardworking place. She wiggled her shoulders, glad that her aching back and stiffness had vanished along with the workshed door.

"You look as if you've been enjoying yourself! What's that big grin for?" Her mother was standing in the doorway to the metalwork gallery.

Maddy glanced at the painting, a little sad now to leave Hilda and Iris behind. She smiled. "I wouldn't exactly call it enjoying myself."

"Well, you seem cheerful enough. We'll definitely have to come back here again. I don't know about you but I'm starving now. Shall we get something to eat?"

Maddy nodded and went to join her, realizing that she was really very hungry too. She looked at her watch and it said half past twelve. She must have been standing there holding that speaker for an hour, while somehow in her mind she'd spent a whole day with the buffer lasses. Was it a phone, a speaker, or a magical key to the past? She shook her head trying to gather her thoughts. Had she really imagined all of that? Her mother had always said she had a good imagination. Her handwriting was still dreadful, but her imagination seemed to be getting better and better.

"Now – where shall we go?"

Maddy didn't hesitate. "Orchard Square."

Her mother smiled. "OK. It's always fun there."

They walked through the great modern

glasshouse called the Winter Gardens and out into the sunshine, past small children squealing as they played in the fountains. At Orchard Square they sat at a table in the sun, outside the café near the clock. Maddy's mother left her there while she went inside to buy drinks and sandwiches.

Maddy sat quietly watching the steady stream of people who trailed through the square. Everything was reassuringly modern. Two girls were busking, collecting coins from passers-by. One had purple hair and strummed on a guitar; the other had tiny plaits that danced about her face as she played a violin. But then a gang of teenagers came noisily towards the café. "Please don't come and sit next to me," Maddy prayed.

But they did come and one of the tallest lads sat down just behind her. She edged her chair away, uncomfortably looking round for another table. But then suddenly from nowhere a voice seemed to tell her, *"You stand yer ground and you'll be fine."*

She lifted her head and looked at the teenagers. They were laughing and talking loudly to each other, showing off their mobile phones on the table in front of them. They weren't taking any notice of her at all.

Maddy took a deep breath and made herself relax again. She looked up at the clock and counted the minutes carefully; it showed one minute to one.

On the street, in front of the clock tower, a man was giving out leaflets, which people didn't want to take. Maddy felt sorry for him. She could see that he was struggling to keep a polite smile on his face.

Then the clock started up, making her jump as usual: *ding-dong, ding-dong.*

Just for a second the buzz of conversation dropped and there was a moment of hush. Even the teenagers turned round, huge grins on their faces. Then came the *chug, chug, chugging* sounds as the doors swung open and the two figures appeared. But for once Maddy was distracted. She could hear the wailing metallic sound of the grinding in the background, but she couldn't take her eyes off a woman who came out of the sweet shop. Maddy stared. The woman carried a tray just like the clown had done the day before and she started throwing little packets of sweets to the children all about her. But to Maddy's surprise she was dressed exactly like the carved figure of the buffer girl on the clock, in a long brown dress and apron, her hair held back in a bun.

The grinding sounds continued and Maddy kept staring as the woman carried her tray around the square towards the café. The teenagers held out their hands to her, playing the fool, laughing wildly and begging for the little free gifts.

"Why, what a load of dafties," the woman joked back at them. "One each – if you behave yourselves! There's a special prize in one of these bags!"

The teenagers rushed to open their packets.

The woman moved on to Maddy's table and, even though Maddy didn't hold out her hand, gave her a small packet.

"Thank you," Maddy said politely.

"No – thank *you*!" said the woman. "A fair day's wage for a fair day's work!" Then she quickly passed on.

Maddy stared after her, open-mouthed. She couldn't believe what she'd heard. Just then the *chug, chug, chug* started up again, a warning that the doors were closing and the buffer girl and grinder were going back inside their cupboards. Maddy looked up just in time to see the buffer girl disappear – and just as before there was a brief moment when the buffer girl looked straight at her. Even more astonishing was that this time she felt sure that the carved wooden lips had parted in a smile.

"Phew – what a queue." Maddy's mother was back with crisps, sandwiches and drinks. "What's this?" She nodded at the small packet on the table.

Maddy shrugged her shoulders. She was having a crazy day, but at least it wasn't boring. "A woman dressed as the buffer girl was giving out free sweets," she told her.

Her mother sat down and looked around the square. "A buffer girl? What fun. Where is she now?"

Maddy looked too, trying to pick her out, but the woman was nowhere to be seen.

"There's a clown over there giving something away," her mother pointed out.

Maddy frowned. Where had the buffer girl gone?

"Open it up!" Maddy's mother suggested eagerly.

So Maddy broke open the little packet and tipped out dolly mixtures into her hand. Then something silvery flashed and she reached inside and pulled out two silver and purple tickets.

"What's that?" Her mother leaned forward over her coffee.

Maddy picked up the tickets and tried to

read what they said, but her hand was shaking and, as usual, the letters just jumped up and down in front of her eyes.

She took a deep breath and tried to calm down, looking carefully at the letters, when at last they clicked into the right order and her lips parted in a big smile – **FREE TICKETS**.

"Two free tickets," she said. "For the Cine Centre. We can get in free to any film showing that we choose."

Her mother clapped her hands together. "Well done!" she cried.

The tall lad with the shaved head on the table behind Maddy's turned round and smiled at her. "Good on ya," he said. "You must be special – you've got the special prize."

Chapter 9

Monday Morning

....

Sunday was a restless day; Maddy packed her
schoolbag ready for Monday, but then she
panicked and unpacked it again, throwing her
pencils and ruler on the floor. On Monday
morning she got up early and carefully
packed the bag again. She got her own
breakfast and, without a word from her
mother, set off and marched up the road to
Upper Forge School. When she got there the
first thing she saw was her picture of the
buffer girls, which was already up on the wall.

She saw Michael's hopeful, friendly face
and the empty place on the other side of his
table, but she ignored him and went to sit
with Samantha and Amy.

Their eyebrows shot up and the girls
looked very surprised. "Blooming cheek!"
Samantha muttered under her breath.

Maddy ignored them and started opening her bag. Amy nudged Samantha with her elbow and then they both exploded into giggles.

Still Maddy ignored them and calmly put out her pencil case and ruler. Samantha watched with a puzzled frown on her face. Then at last she spoke. "You're supposed to sit with the Muppet," she hissed.

Amy continued to giggle, but stopped quickly when Miss Taylor came round giving out worksheets. The teacher saw that Maddy had chosen a different place and opened her mouth to say something, but then seemed to change her mind.

"Do you hear me – Mad Elaine, nutter girl?" Samantha hissed, as Miss Taylor moved away. "You're far too stupid to sit here with us! You go and sit with the Muppet – Mad Elaine!"

"Mad Elaine, Mad Elaine!" Amy began chanting.

Maddy put down her pencil and rubber

and faced them. This was it! If ever she was going to sort them out, this was the moment.

"Don't let them scare you, lass! Stand yer ground!" came Hilda's familiar voice.

"I am not stupid!" Maddy said. It came out rather loud and clear, so that the people around her stopped what they were doing and turned to listen.

"I'm not stupid or mad – I'm dyslexic. And anyone who really knows anything will tell you that dyslexic people are usually clever and bright and often very good at imagining things."

Samantha's mouth dropped open and Amy went very quiet. Everyone around them had gone quiet too and from the corner of her eye Maddy could see that Miss Taylor was standing listening.

She felt her cheeks turn red and sweat break out on her forehead, but she took another breath and went on – this was no time to stop.

"If you're dyslexic like I am, it can be hard to get the hang of reading or writing, and it's hard to get yourself organized too, but you find clever ways of getting round things."

By now the whole class was listening in silence. Maddy almost lost her nerve and turned round to look at Miss Taylor, but the teacher nodded her head. "Say what you want to say, Madeleine," she encouraged.

Maddy gulped and started again. "So – I will sit wherever I want and I will not be called stupid or mad!"

Michael leapt to his feet, punching his fist in the air. "Yes!" he cheered. "Yes! Yes!"

Then Maddy really did lose her nerve and couldn't think of anything else to say. Samantha hung her head, her cheeks very pink, while Amy started to cry very quietly.

What on earth have I done? Maddy wondered.

Everyone turned to Miss Taylor to see what was going to happen next. The teacher had been listening, her face very serious, but now she smiled and nodded her head. "I agree with every word that you've said, Madeleine, and I do hope that the whole class has taken note of it!"

"Yes!" Michael was cheering and shouting again. "Yes! Yes!"

"Yes!" more classmates agreed; a lot of people nodded their heads and then some of them started clapping.

Maddy gulped with relief. At last the noise faded.

"Madeleine will sit wherever she wants," Miss Taylor said. "And now I will call the register and we'll all get on with our work."

They ran through the register with everyone answering very promptly, no noise or chatting in the background. Miss Taylor explained that she wanted them to fill in the worksheets and answer questions about their morning at the Millennium Galleries.

Amy dried her eyes and she and Samantha set to work very quietly. Maddy looked down at her paper, but couldn't seem to settle herself enough to read the questions. She couldn't think straight at all. Suddenly she became aware of somebody standing beside her. It was Michael with his pencil case and paper in his hands and a hopeful look on his face.

"I want to sit here too," he said. "I liked sitting with you."

Maddy grinned at him and moved her chair to make room for him.

Michael sat down with just a glance in Miss Taylor's direction. The teacher nodded her approval, so he picked up his pen and started to work.

Samantha and Amy looked at each other, but said nothing. All the children worked for a while, except for Maddy, who still felt rather shaky. Then Samantha stopped and fumbled beneath the table for a moment. Her hands reappeared clutching a small tube of sweets. She said nothing, but pushed one towards Maddy.

"Thanks," said Maddy, glancing at Miss

Taylor as she put it in her mouth.

Samantha pushed another sweet towards Amy, who took it with a slight hiccup. Then after a moment of hesitation she pushed another one towards Michael. He took it with one of his best smiles.

Maddy managed to breathe a bit more steadily as she sucked away at the sweet. She tried to face the questions on the worksheet, but the letters still wouldn't fall into place and make words.

Michael scratched his head and sighed. He began to read the questions quietly out loud. "Question One – Describe the Millennium Galleries. Question Two – What have you learned about the work of a Sheffield buffer girl?"

Maddy caught her breath and smiled at him with gratitude. She looked at her worksheet again and this time the words fell clearly into place. She picked up her pen – the answer to question two was going to take her quite a long time.

Author's Note

....

The author would like to thank Cara and
Brian McOmish-Hill, and Judy and Ian
Kilner for their help and advice. Also Ann
Chumbley of the Sheffield Galleries and
Museums Trust for her help in gaining
permission from the Bridgeman Art Library
for a line illustration of William Rothenstein's
Buffer Girls, and the staff of Sheffield Local
Studies Library, Central Library, Surrey
Street.

Much of the information about the work of
buffer girls came from *Diamonds in Brown
Paper* by Gill Booth, published by Sheffield
City Libraries, 1988. Also *Back to the
Grindstone* by Herbert Housley, published by
The Hallamshire Press, 1998.

If you visit the Millennium Galleries in
Sheffield, you will see William Rothenstein's

painting of the buffer girls. At the time of writing this story, a shiny metal speaker was fixed beneath the painting. However, all you will find there now is a set of headphones. The speaker has already vanished with the magic of time!

Some more Time-Slip Adventures:

MEET ME BY THE STEELMEN

Theresa Tomlinson

At the heart of Meadowhall shopping centre, the site of the old Sheffield steelworks, stand three giant bronze statues: the steelmen. Stevie, Jenny's younger brother, can't take his eyes off them; he even claims they move and speak. Jenny thinks he's imagining things – and yet there is something strange about the statues. Could it be they're haunted by steelworkers from long ago?

SHORTLISTED FOR THE CARNEGIE MEDAL

NIGHT OF THE RED DEVIL

Theresa Tomlinson

In the middle of a family holiday in Whitby, Sam makes two amazing discoveries: a hidden room behind a door in his wardrobe and a lump of jet on the beach. Together they draw him into an incredible adventure – one that takes him back in time over a hundred years, to the world of the mysterious red devils.

Will Sam change the course of history?

SCAVENGER BOY

Theresa Tomlinson

Michael buys a wooden bobbin the day he moves to his new home in Cromford village. Old and cracked, with the letters FL carved into it, the bobbin rolls backwards and forwards, turning in his hand as if it has a life of its own. Then, one snowy day, Michael finds himself turning too ... and all of a sudden he's back two hundred years among the weavers and their children – the scavengers – working in a local cotton mill.